Justin's Just Joking

SHIRLEY BOGART

Illustrated by Richard Max Kolding

Grolier Enterprises, Inc.,   Danbury, Connecticut

NOTE TO PARENTS

Justin's Just Joking
A story about being considerate of others' feelings

In this story, Justin the Joking Jackal plays practical jokes, pranks, and tricks on his AlphaPet friends. When the AlphaPets decide to turn the tables on him, Justin gets a dose of his own medicine, and realizes that practical jokes are usually more hurtful than funny.

In addition to enjoying this entertaining story with your child, you can use it to teach a gentle lesson about considering people's feelings before playing or telling jokes at their expense. Discuss the difference between laughing *at* people and *with* them.

You can also use this story to introduce the letter **J**. As you read about Justin the Joking Jackal, ask your child to listen for all the **J** words and point to the objects that begin with **J**. When you've finished reading the story, your child will enjoy doing the activity at the end of the book.

The AlphaPets™ characters were conceived and created by Ruth Lerner Perle.
Characters interpreted and designed by Deborah Colvin Borgo.
Cover/book design and production by Norton & Company.
Logo design by Deborah Colvin Borgo and Nancy S. Norton.
Edited by Ruth Lerner Perle.

Emmy
the Exaggerating Elephant

Fenton
the Fearful Frog

Gertie
the Grungy Goat

Herbie
the Happy Hamster

Ivy
the Impatient Iguana

Ollie
the Obedient Ostrich

Perry
the Polite Porcupine

Queenie
the Quiet Quail

Rupert
the Resourceful Rhinoceros

Wendy
the Wise Woodchuck

Xavier
the X-ploring Xenops

Yori
the Yucky Yak

Ziggy
the Zippy Zebra

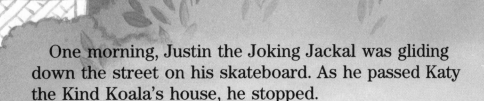

One morning, Justin the Joking Jackal was gliding down the street on his skateboard. As he passed Katy the Kind Koala's house, he stopped.

Justin smiled a funny smile as he ran up the front steps. He rang Katy's door bell, then quickly hid behind the bushes.

When Katy opened the door, she didn't see anyone. She stepped outside and looked around. "Who's there?" she called.

Justin jumped out behind Katy and shouted, "Boo!"

"Oh, Justin," cried Katy. "You shouldn't do that! You really scared me."

"Can't you take a little joke?" said Justin. And he started to laugh.

But Katy didn't laugh.

"Oh, Justin, stop your silly tricks," said Katy. "Come in and have a snack with Connie and me."

Justin followed Katy into the kitchen. He said, "Hi" to Connie the Cuddly Cat, and looked at all the jars of jam and jelly on the counter.

Justin smiled a funny smile. "Why don't you both go into the dining room and I'll bring the food in," he said.

"How kind of you, Justin," Katy said. "Connie and I will set the table. You can bring the crackers, a jar of jam, and the jug of juice."

Just as Connie and Katy sat down at the table, they heard a great crash coming from the kitchen.

"*Ow! Ow! Ow!* My ankle! I really hurt my ankle!" Justin shouted.

Connie ran to the kitchen. Justin was sitting on the floor, holding his foot.

"Oh, you poor thing!" Connie cried.

Katy quickly brought a bowl of ice and some bandages. "What happened?" she asked. "How did you get hurt?"

Justin smiled a funny smile. "I guess I tripped on my shoelace and fell," he said.

"This looks serious, Justin," said Katy. "Your ankle could be broken. I'd better call an ambulance."

Katy picked up the phone and started to dial the emergency number.

Justin jumped up. "Stop! Don't call the ambulance! I was only joking," he shouted. "Fooled you! Fooled you!" and he started to laugh.

Katy hung up the phone. "That's not funny," she said.

"What's the matter?" said Justin. "Can't you take a little joke?"

But Katy and Connie did not laugh. "If you act like that, people won't want to be your friend," said Katy.

The next day, Justin saw Ziggy the Zippy Zebra jogging past his house.

"Hey, Ziggy!" he called. "How about coming in for a game of jacks?"

"I'd like to play jacks with you, Justin," said Ziggy. "But I have to catch the three o'clock train. "I'm going camping with Bradley the Brave Bear this weekend. He's meeting me at the train station with all our camping equipment."

"You have plenty of time to play. It's only twelve o'clock," said Justin.

"Well, all right, I'll play for a little while," Ziggy agreed. "But I have to leave no later than two o'clock. I don't want to miss that train."

When Ziggy came into Justin's house, Justin showed him the clock on the wall. "You'll have no trouble telling what time it is," he said.

"Okay, let's play," Ziggy said, sitting down at the table.

Justin smiled his funny smile. "Ziggy, you take the jacks out of the bag and I'll get some jelly beans to munch on."

When Ziggy wasn't looking, Justin tiptoed over to the clock and moved the clock hands *forward* to make the time look later than it really was.

Justin came back with a jar of jelly beans, and the two friends started to play.

After a while, Justin looked up and asked Ziggy, "What time did you say you had to leave?"

"At two o'clock," Ziggy answered.

Justin pointed to the clock. It said three o'clock.

Ziggy jumped up. "Oh, no!" he cried. "How could it be so late? Now I missed the train and poor Bradley must still be waiting for me." Ziggy started to cry.

"Fooled you! Fooled you!" said Justin. "It's really only two o'clock. You're not late at all." Justin laughed as he moved the clock hands back where they belonged.

"You're not a bit funny," said Ziggy. "You made me feel awful."

"What's the matter?" said Justin. "Can't you take a little joke?"

But Ziggy did not laugh. "If you act like that, Justin, people won't want to play with you," he said.

The next day, Justin had another idea. He invited
Emmy the Exaggerating Elephant and Fenton the Fearful
Frog to a picnic on his lawn.

Justin lead the way to a grassy spot under a shady
juniper tree. Then he handed out the box lunches he
had prepared.

"Peanut butter and jelly sandwiches, apple juice, and
raisins!" said Fenton. "How nice! But I hope the cut
grass won't make me sneeze. I might spill the juice."

"Nonsense!" exclaimed Emmy. "Nothing can stop us
from enjoying this exceptionally elegant treat."

Justin smiled a funny smile. "Hmmm . . ." he said,
scratching his jaw. "Just wait till we get to dessert!"

When they were finished eating, Justin handed Fenton and Emmy another box.

"Now don't open your dessert boxes until I count to three," he said. "Ready? One. Two. *Three!*"

Just as they opened their boxes, wiggly paper snakes jumped out at them!

"*Oh! Yow! Yech!*" the AlphaPets screamed.

"Fooled you! Fooled you!" cried Justin.

"That was *not* funny," said Fenton. "I almost fainted."

"It's only a jack-in-the-box!" said Justin. "Can't you take a little joke?"

But Emmy and Fenton did not laugh.

That evening, the AlphaPets met at Emmy's house.

"We have to do something about Justin and his not-so-funny jokes," said Emmy.

"Yes," Fenton agreed. "We tried to tell him not to play tricks on us, but he just doesn't listen."

"I have an idea," said Ziggy.

Everyone gathered around Ziggy while he told his plan.

The next day, there was an invitation in Justin's mailbox. It said, "Come to a silly costume party at Emmy's house next Saturday. There will be a prize for the silliest costume."

"This will be fun!" thought Justin. "Nobody can be sillier than I am. I know I'll win the prize!"

Justin got busy making his costume. He went up to his attic and gathered some odds and ends together. First, he used a mop and some old hair rollers to make a wig. Then, he attached straps to a trash can to make a tin suit. Next, he used two boxes to make clunky, junky, shoes. Finally, he pinned a trick flower on his jacket.

"I'll be the jolly, jumbled, junk man," he said. "What can be sillier than that?"

On the evening of the party, Justin walked to Emmy's house, clanging and banging every step of the way. He smiled to himself as he wondered what silly costumes the other AlphaPets would be wearing.

When Justin arrived at the house, he rang the bell. Emmy opened the door. She was wearing a pretty party dress and sparkling jewelry.

"Good evening," Emmy said with a chuckle, as Justin entered the room.

Justin looked around. "But nobody's wearing costumes!" he cried. "My invitation said to come to a silly costume party."

"So it did," said Fenton. "But yours was the *only* invitation that said that!"

"Fooled you! Fooled you!" sang the AlphaPets.

"That's not nice! You tricked me," Justin shouted.

"You're right, Justin. It's not nice to trick people or play jokes on them," said Katy.

"We tried to tell you that, but you wouldn't listen," added Ziggy. "We want to be your friends. Maybe now that you know how it feels to be tricked, you won't do it anymore."

Justin started to cry. "I guess it's not so funny when the joke is on me," he said.

Justin began to leave, but Connie stopped him and gave him a hug.

"Don't go," she said. "Stay here with us! And since you have the silliest costume, you do win the prize."

Connie gave Justin a package.

Justin unwrapped the prize. It was a big book of jokes.

"Thank you one and all," said Justin, smiling a happy smile. "And now, I have a little joke for you . . ."

"Knock, knock."

"Who's there?" asked the AlphaPets.

"Justin."

"Justin, who?" they asked.

"*Just in* time to enjoy the party with all my friends," said Justin.

This time *everybody* laughed.

Let's have fun with these words—no joking.

jar

jewelry

GRAPE
JELLY

jelly

jacks

jelly beans

jump rope

jam

juice

jacket

Look back at the pictures in this book and find these and other things that begin with the letter J.

Aa Bb

Gg Hh

Mm Nn Oo Pp

Uu Vv Ww